GALAXY ZACK

THREE'S A CROWD!

By Ray O'Ryan
Illustrated by Colin Jack

LITTLE SIMON
New York   London   Toronto   Sydney   New Delhi

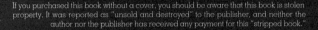 LITTLE SIMON

An imprint of Simon & Schuster Children's Publishing Division
1230 Avenue of the Americas, New York, New York 10020
Copyright © 2013 by Simon & Schuster, Inc.
All rights reserved, including the right of reproduction in whole or in part in any form. LITTLE SIMON is a registered trademark of Simon & Schuster, Inc., and associated colophon is a trademark of Simon & Schuster, Inc. For information about special discounts for bulk purchases, please contact Simon & Schuster Special Sales at 1-866-506-1949 or business@simonandschuster.com.
The Simon & Schuster Speakers Bureau can bring authors to your live event. For more information or to book an event contact the Simon & Schuster Speakers Bureau at 1-866-248-3049 or visit our website at www.simonspeakers.com.
Initial interior sketches by Andrew Murray
Designed by Nicholas Sciacca
Manufactured in the United States of America 0813 FFG
First Edition 10 9 8 7 6 5 4 3 2 1
Library of Congress Cataloging-in-Publication Data
O'Ryan, Ray.
Three's a crowd! / by Ray O'Ryan ; illustrated by Colin Jack. — First edition.
pages cm. — (Galaxy Zack ; 5)
Summary: "Zack is thrilled when his best friend on Earth, Bert Jones, visits for the weekend. But when Zack introduces Bert to Drake, his best friend on Nebulon, trouble begins!" — Provided by publisher.
ISBN 978-1-4424-8221-0 (pbk. : alk. paper) — ISBN 978-1-4424-8222-7 (hardcover : alk. paper) — ISBN 978-1-4424-8223-4 (ebook : alk. paper) [1. Science fiction. 2. Best friends—Fiction. 3. Friendship—Fiction. 4. Human-alien encounters—Fiction.] I. Jack, Colin, illustrator. II. Title.
PZ7.O7843Th 2013
[Fic]—dc23
2012038974

CONTENTS

Chapter 1
Waiting for Bert

Zack Nelson jumped up from his seat at the kitchen table. He had hardly taken a bite from the stack of nebucakes that sat on his plate.

"I can't believe he's coming today!" Zack cried. He threw both his arms into the air. Then he spun around in a circle

1

and shouted, "YIPPEE WAH-WAH!"

"Honey, I know you're excited that Bert is coming to visit," said Shelly Nelson, Zack's mom. "But you haven't touched any of your breakfast. Nebu-cakes with boingoberry syrup are your favorite. And it's almost time to leave for school."

"But *Bert* is coming!" Zack shouted. "I haven't seen him in so long!"

Bert Jones was Zack's best friend on Earth. But Zack didn't live on Earth anymore. A few months ago Zack and his family had moved to the planet Nebulon. Zack had not seen Bert since he moved.

3

At least not in person.

Sure they kept in touch through z-mail and video chats. Zack even had a holocam that showed a 3-D image of Bert. It almost felt like Bert was in the room.

But not really.

Zack missed going to baseball games with Bert. He missed

trading 3-D holo-comics. He missed going to the orbiting drive-in movie

theater for triple features. He just missed having his best buddy nearby, even if they had nothing to do.

Zack missed Bert. And now Bert was coming from Earth to visit him on Nebulon. Zack couldn't wait to show Bert around his new home planet.

"Come on, honey. You have to eat something!" Mom insisted.

Zack leaned over his plate. He grabbed an entire nebu-cake and shoved it into his mouth. A thin line of purple boingoberry syrup ran down his chin.

"Dmvrum barimden," he mumbled through a mouthful of food.

"Don't talk with your mouth full," said Mom.

Zack swallowed.

"Okay," he said. "Gotta go. Can't be late for school. The Sprockets Speedybus will be here any second. Bye, Mom!"

"Have a good day at school," Mom said.

Zack grabbed his jacket and his backpack and dashed out the front door. His twin sisters, Charlotte and Cathy, followed him outside.

"Bye, Mom. . . ."

"We'll see you . . ."

". . . after school," said Charlotte and Cathy.

The school speedybus was waiting outside.

Now all I have to do is make it through the school day! Zack thought. Then he and his sisters climbed on board the bus.

Chapter 2
Best Friends

Zack sat in his classroom at Sprockets Academy. He did his best to pay attention. His teacher, Ms. Rudolph, stood in front of the class. Her lesson was about the great Nebulon scientist Renur Lelo. Lelo had made many discoveries about Nebulon's two suns and three moons.

"Renur Lelo tracked shadows on Nebulon and also those cast on the moons. That is how she made her amazing discoveries," Ms. Rudolph explained.

Normally, Zack was very interested in science. But today all he could think about was Bert. He looked at his Galactic Standard watch.

Only nine more hours until Bert arrives! Wait until I tell Drake. He's going to be so excited!

Zack worked hard all morning to concentrate. Finally, lunchtime arrived. Zack hurried to the space bus that took students to the cafeteria. He found a seat next to Drake.

Ever since Zack and his family moved from Earth to Nebulon, Drake Taylor had been his best new friend.

"Today's the day, Drake!" Zack said excitedly.

"The day for what, Zack?" asked Drake.

"The day that Bert is coming!" Zack

shouted. "Remember? Bert is my best friend from Earth. He's landing at the Creston City Spaceport this evening. Then tomorrow he's coming to school with me!"

"That should be fun," said Drake— although it didn't *sound* like Drake thought it would be fun.

"Oh yeah, Bert is tons of fun!" said Zack. "He likes baseball and amusement parks and exploring and dogs and burgers and fries and all kinds of grape stuff." On Nebulon, grape means "cool." After living on Nebulon for a few months, Zack started using this term too.

"I am sure you guys will have a good time," said Drake.

"Yeah, we will," replied Zack. "After all, Bert is my best friend!"

Drake nodded, then looked out the window.

Drake doesn't seem like himself today, thought Zack. *Usually he's super-excited about everything.*

The space bus soon arrived at the
cafeteria. Zack was hungry for lunch,
so he hurried off. Drake walked slowly
behind him.

Chapter 3
Bert's Here!

After school, Zack climbed into the Nelson family's flying car. His mom was in the driver's seat.

"I told Drake all about Bert today," Zack said excitedly.

"Oh yeah?" said Mom.

"I told him about all the grape

stuff Bert and I used to do on Earth," explained Zack. "Bert is so cool, I just know that Drake is going to like him."

"And what did Drake have to say?" asked Mom.

"Not much," admitted Zack. "But he's *got* to like Bert. After all, Bert is my best friend."

A few minutes later the Creston
City Spaceport
came into view.

The complex was huge. It spread out

for miles in every direction.
All kinds of ships zoomed
in and out of
the spaceport. Some
ships were small
private spacecrafts.
Others were public shuttles.

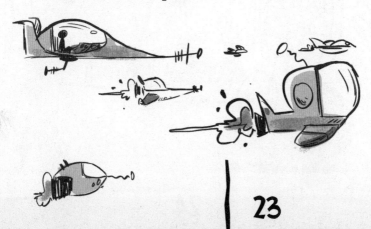

23

After Mom landed the flying car, they walked over to the waiting area of the spaceport. Many different-looking kinds of people hurried

WAITING AREA
PLEASE ENJOY WAITING

around the terminal. Some were tall and very thin and had red skin. Others were long and round and crawled on the ground on many tiny legs.

Some people hurried to catch ships
that were taking off for far distant planets. Others ran to meet loved ones who
had just landed.

Zack pulled out
his hyperphone.
He pressed a
button. A list of
arriving flights
appeared on
the screen.

"Flight six-two-five from Earth to Nebulon is scheduled to land in five minutes!" he said. Then he jumped up and down with excitement.

Zack paced back and forth. Every few seconds he looked up at the giant

holographic clock on the spaceport's ceiling. The second hand that *tick-tick-ticked* floated in midair.

"Zack, pacing is not going to make Bert get here faster," Mom pointed out.

Zack stopped pacing. Then he immediately started again.

"Flight six-two-five from Earth is now arriving at landing pod fifty-one," said an announcement over the space-port's loudspeakers.

"That's it!" Zack shrieked. "He's
here!"

Zack walked quickly around the
spaceport. He came to a round door
with a number above it. An electronic
buzzer sounded. The number fifty-one

lit up. Then the door slid open.

A crowd of people rushed through
the door.

Then Zack spotted Bert.

"Hey, Bert!" he shouted. "Over here!"

Chapter 4
Welcome to Nebulon!

Bert hurried over to Zack. He dropped his backpack onto the floor.

Before either one said a word, they both launched into their special handshake. First they gave each other high fives with their right hands. Then with their left hands. They each lifted a fist into the air and bumped them together. Then the two friends started laughing.

Zack noticed a few Nebulites staring at the two of them.

"It's so cool that you're here!" said Zack.

"Don't you mean 'so grape'?" said Bert.

Zack had told Bert about the word "grape" in one of their many 3-D holo-chats.

They both laughed.

Mom joined the two boys.

"Hello, Bert! It's so nice to see you," she said with a smile. "How was your flight?"

"It was good, Mrs. Nelson. Thanks," replied Bert.

"Before we do anything, please z-mail your mom and dad to let them know you arrived safely," said Mom. "And say hello for me."

Bert sent a quick message to his parents. Then they headed to the car.

"I know you told me that Nebulites are blue," Bert whispered. "But it's amazing to see them in person. Their arms and legs are so long and skinny."

"Yeah," replied Zack. "There are all kinds of cool people on Nebulon."

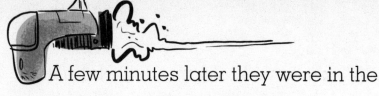

A few minutes later they were in the car and flying toward home.

Bert stared in amazement at all the flying cars zooming past them.

"Wow!" he exclaimed. "Nebulon is like something out of a movie!"

"Told ya!" said Zack. He was proud of his new home planet. He was also thrilled to have his best friend at his side.

When they landed at home, Zack's dog, Luna, bounded from the house and jumped on Bert.

"Hi, Luna!" said Bert, rubbing her head. "It's good to see you, girl."

Bert had taken care of Luna during the time the Nelson family made their move from Earth to Nebulon.

"Come on inside," said Zack. "Wait until you see my house!"

Zack hurried over to a round door in the garage. The door slid open and he stepped into the elevator. Bert, Mom, and Luna followed him in.

"Which room is this?" asked Bert.

"It's not a room, it's an elevator!" Zack said, smiling. He remembered the first time he had stepped into this elevator. And he remembered what came next.

Chapter 5

Home, Sweet Home!

The elevator door closed with a soft hiss. Then the elevator started moving—sideways.

"Whoa!" exclaimed Bert. "This reminds me of a ride we used to go on at the Low Gravity Amusement Park on Venus."

"Our elevator can take you to all the sections of the house," Zack said proudly. "It moves through tubes or something. It can go sideways, up, down, forward, and backward."

Zack recalled how nervous he had been about moving away from Earth. He thought about how strange this new house felt when he first walked in. Now he was showing it off to Bert. This really had become his home.

The elevator glided to a stop. The doors slid open.

Zack, Bert, Mom, and Luna stepped into the kitchen.

"Wow! This kitchen looks like something from a spaceship!" said Bert.

Shiny counters and glass panels lined the whole room.

"Hey, Bert! Welcome to our home!" said Otto Nelson, Zack's dad. "What do you think?"

"Hi, Mr. Nelson," replied Bert. "You have a really cool house here."

"You haven't seen anything yet," said Dad.

"It *is* quite a house," Mom said.

"Welcome home, Master Just Zack," said Ira, the Nelson's Indoor Robotic Assistant. "And you must be Bert. Zack has talked about you ever since he moved here."

"Uh, who just said that?" asked Bert, looking around. "I don't see anybody else."

"That's Ira," Zack

47

explained. "He's built into the house.
Ira controls everything—the comput-
ers, the communications systems, all
the electronic and mechanical parts
of the house."

"This *is* like a spaceship!" said Bert.

"Oh, and I forgot the best part," Zack
added quickly. "Are you hungry?"

"I'm starving! All they served on the

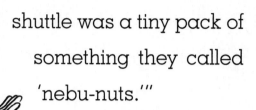

shuttle was a tiny pack of something they called 'nebu-nuts.'"

"No problem," said Zack. "What do you feel like eating?"

"I'd love a burger and fries," said Bert.

"On Nebulon we call that a galactic patty and crispy fritters," explained Zack. "Ira, two galactic patties and two crispy fritters, please."

"Certainly, Master Just Zack," said Ira.

"What does 'Master Just Zack' mean?" Bert whispered.

Zack laughed. "I'll tell you later," he said. "Let's sit in the dining room."

A panel in the ceiling slid open. Two plates of food floated down before Zack and Bert.

"Two galactic patties and crispy fritters," said Ira.

"You mean all you have to do is tell Ira what you want, and food just appears?" Bert asked.

"Pretty much," replied Zack.

"I think I could get used to life on Nebulon!" said Bert.

Bert took a bite of his galactic patty.

"Mmmm, this is really good! Thanks, Ira!"

"You're welcome, Master Bert," said Ira.

"Would you like something to drink?" asked Zack.

"Can Ira make a shake?" Bert asked.

"Ira, two boingoberry cosmic coolers, please!" Zack requested.

Two bubbling purple drinks dropped down from the ceiling.

Bert took a sip. "This is delicious too!" he exclaimed. He wiped the purple mustache from his mouth.

When they had finished eating, the boys hurried to Zack's room.

Zack had a huge desk. A computer touch pad was built into the desktop. The entire wall behind the desk was a giant view screen.

"Touch the top of the desk," Zack said to Bert.

Bert tapped the desktop with his finger. Billions of stars swirling through space suddenly appeared on the screen.

"This is even better than the über-zoom galactic telescope you had on Earth!" shouted Bert.

"I know!" said Zack. "You can see the whole galaxy from right here! And, hey, check out the beds!"

"Two beds coming right up," said
Ira.

A panel in the ceiling opened and
two fully made beds dropped down
from above.

"I don't even have to make my bed
every morning!" said Zack.

"Super-cool!" said Bert.

"And tomorrow, you can come to school with me!" said Zack.

Zack and Bert went to the family room and settled down in front of the sonic cell monitor, the Nebulon version of TV. They watched a few quins of a galactic blast game. Then it was time to go to sleep. Both boys got into their beds for the night and looked forward to the next day.

Chapter 6
Bert at Sprockets

Zack's mom dropped the kids off at Sprockets Academy the next morning. The two boys scrambled out of the car.

"Have a great day, guys," said Mom. "And Zack?"

Zack hung back for a moment. "Don't forget to introduce Bert to

Ms. Rudolph and your friends."

"Sure, Mom!" said Zack.

The boys ran toward the school's entrance.

Zack spotted Drake.

"Hey, Drake, wait up!" he shouted.

Drake spun around.

"Drake, this is Bert," Zack said. "My best friend from Earth. He's coming to class with us today. Bert, this is Drake, my new friend here on Nebulon."

Drake lifted his hand with his palm facing out. He moved his hand in a small circle in front of his face.

"Nice to meet you, Bert," said Drake.

"Zack has told me a lot about you."

Bert raised his hand and made a circle in front of his face.

"Nice to meet you too, Drake," he said. "Zack told me how Nebulites shake hands. It's pretty cool. Or, actually, pretty grape!"

Zack led Bert into the classroom

and over to his teacher.

"Ms. Rudolph, this is my friend Bert from Earth," Zack explained. "He'd like to sit in our class today."

"That's very nice," said Ms. Rudolph. "Welcome, Bert. I'm from Earth too."

"You are?" Bert asked.

"Yes. And I think that once you get to know

Nebulon, you'll love it as much as I do,"
Ms. Rudolph said. "Now, please find a
seat, and let's begin today's lessons."

Zack pointed to two empty seats.
"Over here," he said to Bert.

The two boys sat down.

"Wow! What's this?" Bert asked. He
pointed to a large screen right in front
of him.

"That's your edu-screen," Zack
explained. "Just tap it in the center."

Bert tapped the screen and a series
of images blazed to life. One showed
a picture of an ancient civilization.

Another showed a close-up of an atom. A third showed a series of mathematical equations.

"Everyone, please open your science holo-text," said Ms. Rudolph.

Zack leaned over and tapped the atom on Bert's screen. The rest of the images disappeared and the 3-D atom rose higher from the desk. It spun around in the air right in front of their eyes.

"Now *that* is grape!" whispered Bert.

Chapter 7
Lunchtime

As the school day continued, Zack helped Bert follow all the lessons. When the bell rang for lunch, Zack led Bert to the space bus.

Zack and Bert sat next to each other. Drake sat in the seat behind Zack.

"What an amazing way to learn

your lessons," Bert said. "It's like history, science, and everything else comes alive right before your eyes."

A few minutes later, the space bus arrived at the cafeteria. Zack, Bert, and Drake hurried in, along with all the other kids.

"Let's grab a table," said Zack. The three boys sat down at a small round table.

Bert looked around.

"Hey, where's the lunch line?" he asked. "Where's all the food?"

Drake smiled. "I think you asked me the same thing on your first day, Zack," he said.

"There's no lunch line," said Zack. "Check this out!"

A long line of robots came walking into the cafeteria. They had metal bodies of all shapes and sizes. Each robot pushed a cart filled with food.

"Do you have galactic patties and crispy fritters?" Bert asked a robot.

The robot handed Bert a plate with exactly what he had asked for.

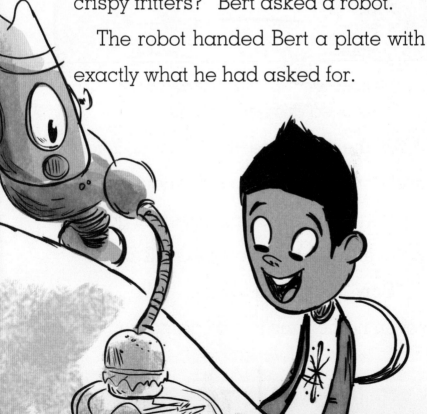

"This is so grape!" he said.

As the boys ate their lunch, Zack and Bert continued to talk about Earth.

"Remember the first baseball game we ever went to?" Bert asked Zack.

"Sure," replied Zack. "We saw seven home runs in one game!"

"Baseball," said Drake. "That's like Galactic Blast except that people—not robots—play. Right, Zack?"

"Yup," said Zack. Then he turned back to Bert.

"Remember that time in gym back on Earth?" Zack asked Bert.

Both boys started laughing. Bert knew exactly what Zack was talking about.

"You mean when Percy Lewis kicked the ball so hard that he fell back and landed on his behind?" Bert asked.

"Yup," replied Zack, laughing. "You should have seen it, Drake. And to top it off—Bert caught the ball, so

Percy was out of the game anyway!"

Zack and Bert fell into a giggling fit.

"Sounds pretty funny," said Drake.

But he wasn't laughing.

Zack and Bert talked and laughed about their days together on Earth. But Drake stayed quiet. He felt lost in their conversation.

Then the bell rang, ending lunch. All three boys got back on the space bus.

When Zack and Bert sat down in
a seat together, Drake didn't try to sit
near them.

"Hey, Drake!" Zack called. "Where
are you going?"

Drake didn't answer.

That's strange, Zack thought.
*Maybe he doesn't feel well after that
lunch.* Zack shrugged and turned his
attention back to Bert.

Chapter 8
A New Adventure!

That night at dinner, Dad had a big surprise for Zack and Bert.

"How would you like to go to the planet Cisnos tomorrow?" he asked. "I figured since Bert is visiting we would do something special on Saturday."

"Oh wow! Isn't that where the

Lollyland Amusement Park is?" Zack asked excitedly.

"You bet!" said Dad.

"What's that?" Bert asked.

"I haven't been there yet," Zack explained. "But Drake has, and he told me it was awesome!"

"And I've already spoken with Drake's parents," Dad continued. "He's coming with us!"

"That's great!" cried Zack. "Bert, you and I are going to go on every ride there!"

"And we can play games," added Bert. "Maybe even win a prize!"

"We're going to have the best time," said Zack. "Thanks, Dad!"

"Don't forget to include Drake in your fun tomorrow, Zack," said Mom.

"I know, Mom," said Zack. Then he turned back to Bert.

"Maybe they'll have a super-long slide!" said Zack.

"And bumper cars!" added Bert. "This is going to be great!"

Zack and Bert hardly slept that night. They were so excited about their trip to Lollyland, they talked and talked through most of the night.

Zack, Bert, and Dad headed to the Creston City Spaceport the next morning. There they met Drake.

"Okay then, let's get on board the Cisnos shuttle!" said Dad.

A few minutes later they were all buckled into their seats on the shuttle.

There were several Cisnosians on the same shuttle. They were all short and a lot wider than humans or Nebulites. They had orange hair and their skin was slightly orange in color too! The ship took off with a loud roar. Then, once again, Zack was in space.

"I love space travel," Zack said. He looked out the window. "Check out all those stars!"

"I love space travel too," said Bert. "And I'm so excited about seeing another planet! That'll make two new planets in just a few days."

"The planet Cisnos is very interest-
ing," said Drake. "Did you know that
the people who live there are all less
than four feet tall?"
"Really?"
said Dad.

"Yes, and their favorite food is called cisnosi," Drake continued. "It's a mix between pizza and pasta."

"I can't wait to get to Lollyland!" cried Bert.

"Me too!" said Zack, not hearing the fun facts Drake was sharing.

"Actually, Lollyland has more than twenty-five rides," Drake said. "I have been on ten of them. My favorite is the—"

"I hope they have a roller coaster!" Zack said, interrupting Drake.

"I hope they have a fun house!" said Bert.

Drake slumped down in his seat and stayed quiet for the rest of the trip.

Chapter 9
Lollyland!

The shuttle approached Cisnos. Zack and Bert were amazed because when they looked down, the entire surface of the planet looked orange.

"That is because of the orange mountains that cover most of the planet," Drake explained.

Houses and towns came into view.

"The houses are round," said Zack. "And they look like they are made of clay."

"Actually they are made of cron-dike," Drake added. "It is a substance found in the mountains. It is easy to build with and not expensive."

The shuttle dropped down into the spaceport. Zack looked around at all the people. They looked like humans, except they were much shorter and they all had orange hair.

"Is that really the color of their hair?" Bert asked.

95

"It is," replied Drake.

The shuttle finally landed. The boys and Mr. Nelson hopped into a space taxi, which brought them to Lollyland.

The amusement park spread out in front of them like a magical city. Brightly lit rides rose high into the sky.

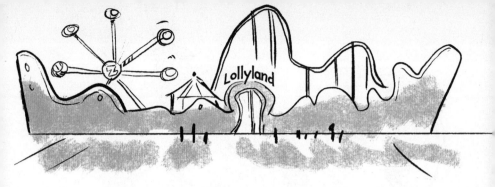

"Look at this place!" exclaimed Bert. "It's like something from another planet!"

"It *is* from another planet!" Zack pointed out. Then he and Bert cracked up.

"Okay, guys, which ride would you like to go on first?" Dad asked.

Zack looked around.

"That one!" he shouted. Zack pointed at a ride that looked like a giant flashing wheel with a round car attached to the end of each spoke. Each car also spun around in a circle.

"That is the Zeppler," explained Drake. "It is one of my favorites."

"Great," said Dad. "You boys get in line. I'm going to grab something to eat."

Zack, Bert, and Drake hurried over to the line for the Zeppler. After a short wait, they reached the front of the line.

"Okay, who's next?" shouted the Cisnosian man who ran the ride. He was shorter than all the boys and appeared to be about three feet wide.

"Come on, Zack!" Bert shouted, racing toward one of the cars. "Let's get in the green car—green is your favorite color!"

Zack and Drake ran over to the green car. But when they got there they discovered that each car only held two people. Zack looked at Drake. He was not sure what to do.

"Go ahead, Zack," said Drake. "You go in the green car with Bert. I will get in the next car."

"Thanks, Drake!" said Zack. He

scrambled into the green car. Drake climbed into a red car right behind them.

The ride began. All the cars lifted into the air. Then they began spinning.

"Wooooo!" Bert and Zack screamed together.

"This ride is the BEST!" Zack shouted as the world spun around and around.

After a few minutes the cars

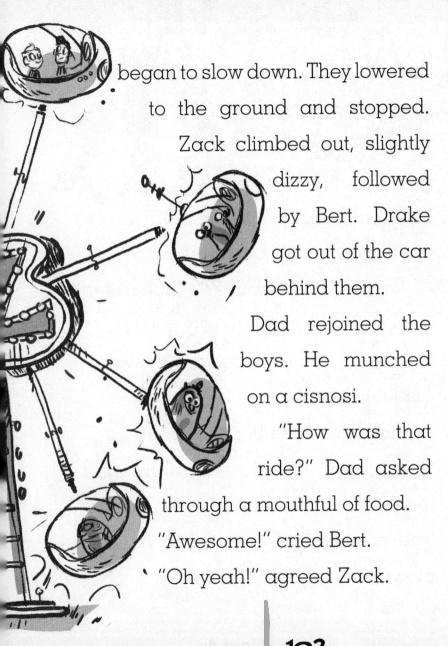

began to slow down. They lowered to the ground and stopped. Zack climbed out, slightly dizzy, followed by Bert. Drake got out of the car behind them.

Dad rejoined the boys. He munched on a cisnosi.

"How was that ride?" Dad asked through a mouthful of food.

"Awesome!" cried Bert.

"Oh yeah!" agreed Zack.

"I had fun too," said Drake.

"What's next?" Dad asked.

"Is there a fun house?" Zack asked Drake. "I love all those silly mirrors."

"On Cisnos it's called the Kaliwog," explained Drake.

"Let's go!" said Bert.

The boys rushed to the Kaliwog. It looked like an old run-down house. The outside was covered in painted clown faces.

"I'll meet you back here when you finish going through the Kaliwog," said Dad.

The boys entered the house. As they walked down a narrow hallway, the ceiling got lower and lower. By they time they reached the end of the hall they were crawling on their bellies.

"This is pretty cool," said Bert.

"I love it!" cried Zack.

They walked into another room. The whole room was crooked. It tilted to one side. Zack took a step forward. He started sliding across the floor.

A silly Wooooooo sound rang out as all three boys slid across the crooked room and fell down.

The boys all got to their feet.

"Wait until you see the mirrors," said Drake.

He pulled open a door.

Out popped a giant clown head that startled them all.

"This place is full of surprises," said Bert.

The boys walked through the door. The room they were in was filled with mirrors that were curved in all different ways. Each one created a different weird image.

"This one makes me look like a pro football player!" said Zack.

"And this one makes me look like a skinny giant!" said Bert, standing up tall.

"Hey, guys. Look at my funny faces in this mirror," said Drake. "This is great. Watch."

Drake stuck his fingers into his mouth and pulled his cheeks open wide. He scrunched up his eyes. His image in the mirror made him look like a weird monster.

"How grape was that, Za—?"

When Drake turned around, Bert and Zack were gone. They had

moved farther into the Kaliwog without him.

Drake wandered through the rest of the fun house alone.

When Drake stepped out of the fun house, he saw Bert and Zack laughing.

"Wasn't that awesome, Drake?" asked Zack.

"I do not want to go on any more rides today," Drake said. "You two go on alone." Zack and Bert stood and watched as Drake walked away.

Chapter 10
Two Best Friends

Dad went over to Zack and Bert. He had seen Drake walk away.

"Drake doesn't want to go on any more rides, Dad," said Zack.

"Zack, I know it's hard to juggle being friends with both Bert and Drake," said Dad. "After all, you have different things in common with each of them. But maybe you can try harder to include Drake? Don't forget, it was Drake who reached out to you when you first moved to Nebulon."

Zack thought about all the ways he had not included Drake—in school, on the shuttle to Cisnos, on the Zeppler, and in the fun house.

"I didn't even realize that I was leaving Drake out," said Zack, "but now I see that I was wrong." Zack saw Drake ahead, looking at people laughing and having fun on the Slosher ride. Zack ran after him. Bert followed.

"Drake, wait up!" Zack shouted.

Zack and Bert caught up to Drake.

"I'm really sorry I've been leaving you out," said Zack. "It's not fair."

"I'm glad you came with us," said Bert. "You know, Zack talks about you all the time. He's told me all kinds of cool stuff. In fact, before I got to

Nebulon, I was jealous of you, Drake!"

"Really?" Drake asked.

"Yeah," replied Bert. "I thought you had replaced me as Zack's best friend."

"I didn't know that's what you thought, Bert," said Zack.

"I'm just lucky to have two great friends like you guys."

Drake smiled. So did Bert.

"So, who wants to go on another ride?" Zack asked.

"I do!" Bert and Drake both shouted.

"How about the Slosher?" Drake

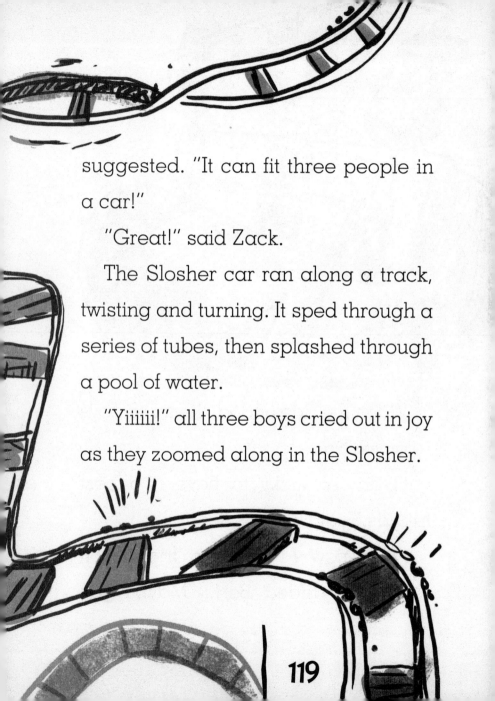

suggested. "It can fit three people in a car!"

"Great!" said Zack.

The Slosher car ran along a track, twisting and turning. It sped through a series of tubes, then splashed through a pool of water.

"Yiiiiii!" all three boys cried out in joy as they zoomed along in the Slosher.

When the ride ended, the three boys rejoined Dad.

"I am so lucky to have *two* best friends," said Zack.

"And now *I* have two friends on Nebulon!" added Bert. "Maybe you and Zack can both visit me on Earth some day."

"I would like that, Bert," said Drake. "Thank you."

"So who's ready for some cisnosi?" Dad asked.

"We are!" the boys shouted. Then they all headed to the cisnosi stand.

CHECK OUT THE NEXT

GALAXY ZACK

ADVENTURE!

HERE'S A SNEAK PEEK!

Zack had trouble sleeping that night. Every few minutes he checked to see if the storm had started.

He finally dozed off.

When Zack woke up, the sky was filled with dark gray clouds. He joined his family at the kitchen table.

An excerpt from *A Green Christmas!*

"It's kinda scary-looking out there," said Zack.

"I was just watching the sonic cell," said Dad. "They expect the storm to hit at any moment."

After breakfast the Nelsons gathered in their living room. Mom and Dad sat on the couch. Cathy and Charlotte curled up on their cozy blanket on the rug. Zack sat in his favorite chair. Luna stretched out on the floor.

Suddenly the room got very dark. Zack looked out the big living room window. The sky had turned from gray to solid black.

An excerpt from A Green Christmas!

A whistling noise screeched outside. The wind picked up.

"It's starting," Zack said softly.

The house began to shake. Windows rattled. Pictures on the wall swung back and forth. A wind-blown tree scraped against the side of the house. Luna yelped and jumped up into Zack's lap.

"It's okay, Luna," said Zack.

But Zack was getting frightened too.

A few minutes later the wind died down. Things got weirdly quiet. Zack ran to the window and could not believe what he was seeing.

An excerpt from *A Green Christmas!*